# TROLLS & galore

## POEMS ABOUT
## FANTASTIC CREATURES

SIMON & SCHUSTER BOOKS FOR YOUNG READERS

Pointed people are six to twelve inches high, wear peaked caps, and have furry brown ears, bright eyes, hooves, and pointed faces. They emerge at dusk and love to play in the shadows, where they are sometimes seen "shaking with silent laughter."

An imp is a small devil who is capable of all manner of things . . .

Gnomes are earth dwellers and live underground, moving freely through the earth as though it were air. They are the guardians of earth's treasures, and as keepers of nature make their rounds to care for earth, air, fire, and water.

Faery folk describes all manner of magical, supernatural, and enchanted creatures.

# CONTENTS

Mr. Nobody is exactly one foot tall with a long coat, a pointed hat, and bare feet . . . or so they say. Always on the move, and rarely seen except from behind as he scurries around a corner or flies out a window, Mr. Nobody is sometimes heard as a faint sound of laughter that hangs in the air just before he disappears.

An ogre is a hideous giant who likes to snack on human beings.

Leprechaun is an Irish word describing a "one shoe-maker" as he is most often observed working on just one shoe. These merry fellows are pigmy-sized, mischievous, and generally wear green clothes, leather aprons, and shoes with silver buckles.

Pixies are small folk but are capable of changing size. They have pointed ears, red hair, and turned up noses. Pixies steal horses at night and love to play pranks on humans, frequently leading travelers astray. They, too, love to wear green.

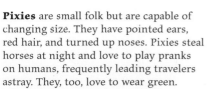

**Goblins** are evil and dangerous. They are small and stocky, often hairy, and always ugly, with large noses and big mouths. However one branch of the goblin family is friendlier: The Knockers live in the tin mines of Devon and Cornwall, and they used to knock to lead miners to rich veins of ore.

**Fairies** are enchanted beings who can shape shift. There are many different kinds of fairies, including the tiny, winged flower fairies, who make flowers grow faster as they dance in fairy rings, and the three- to four-foot fairies, who live in fairy hills and may steal human babies, replacing them with changelings of their own. Most fairies possess magical powers . . . Faery folk are everywhere.

**Trolls** are mischievous beings who can be small and wizened or as tall as giants. Other trolls are human sized and tend to wear gray. They wander about from sunset till dawn, then retreat below ground away from the light. The gigantic trolls are much more vulnerable to daylight; sunlight will turn them to stone.

Unlike their goblin brothers, most **hobgoblins** are good humored. They like to have fun and are fond of practical jokes. However, if humans annoy them in any way, they can become extremely dangerous.

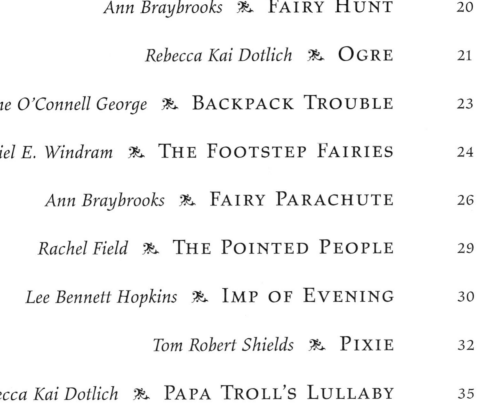

The **banshee** is an Irish death spirit who wails for the ancient families. With long flowing hair and red eyes from continually weeping, she is quite terrifying to look upon. She wears a green dress and gray cloak. She appears when someone is going to die.

A **leshy** is a Russian nature spirit. They can change shape and form to become the tallest tree, or the smallest blade of grass. And they can imitate any sound the forest may make. But usually they are human-shaped, pale with green eyes, a green beard, and long straggly hair.

There are two kinds of **elves**. The more sinister group steals humans. The smaller fairy-like elves are friendlier, although they sometimes enjoy a harmless prank, and they love to play.

**Spriggans** are the faery bodyguard, protecting treasure within the hills. They are grotesque, ugly little creatures, who are capable of growing very large and changing shape. Some believe they are the ghosts of old giants. Beware of them, for they are dangerous thieves and kidnappers.

# EVIDENCE ✿ *Susan Katz*

Who says there aren't Little People?

Everywhere I've looked, I've found
Lots of stuff they left lying around.

Under the arbor, this folded blue rag
Must be a leprechaun's sleeping bag.

And the tiny red feather I spied in a crack?
It surely fell off a pixie's cap.

The mossy scraps on the garden stair?
A leshy was trimming his green beard there.

The raspberry lying on top of a wall?
An elf kid's soccer team lost their ball.

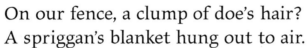

On our fence, a clump of doe's hair?
A spriggan's blanket hung out to air.

And the grayish cobweb under the oak?
A scrap torn off a banshee's cloak.

Who says there aren't Little People?

# HOW TO TELL GOBLINS FROM ELVES ❧ *Monica Shannon*

The Goblin has a wider mouth
    Than any wondering elf.
The saddest part of this is that
    He brings it on himself.
For hanging in a willow clump
    In baskets made of sheaves,
You may see the baby goblins
    Under coverlets of leaves.

They suck a pink and podgy foot
    (As human babies do),
And then they suck the other one,
    Until they're sucking two.
And so it is that goblins' mouths
    Keep growing very round.
So you can't mistake a goblin,
    When a goblin you have found.

# Down Below the Barlor Bridge ❧ *Rebecca Kai Dotlich*

Down below the Barlor bridge
there lives a lonely troll
who guzzles gizzards by the jug,
and beetles by the bowl.

He waits below the Barlor bridge
for someone just like you
to share his scrumptious supper with
(for trolling friends are few).

So if one day you're so inclined
to go below for dinner,
I guarantee that you will be
at least a wee pound thinner.

## MR. NOBODY ✖ *Anonymous*

I know a funny little man,
   As quiet as a mouse,
Who does the mischief that is done
   In everybody's house!
There's no one ever sees his face,
   And yet we all agree
That every plate we break was cracked
   By Mr. Nobody.

'Tis he who always tears our books,
   Who leaves the door ajar,
He pulls the buttons from our shirts,
   And scatters pins afar;
That squeaking door will always squeak,
   For, prithee, don't you see,
We leave the oiling to be done
   By Mr. Nobody.

The finger marks upon the door
   By none of us are made;
We never leave the blinds unclosed,
   To let the curtains fade.
The ink we never spill; the boots
   That lying round you see
Are not our boots—they all belong
   To Mr. Nobody.

# THE FAIRY RING

*Constance Andrea Keremes*

Toss aside your shoes and stockings,
　　Cap and jacket, too,
Clothe yourself in moonbeams
　　Buttoned up with mountain dew.

Let the fairies take your hands
　　And spirit you away,
To a place beyond all time,
　　Where sprite and elf folk play.

Frisk about and twist about,
　　Come join the fairy ring,
Gambol to the tinny tune
　　That toad and cricket sing.

Dip and trip around the circle,
　　Sashay left then right,
Frolic with the little people,
　　Dance away the night.

And when daybreak comes at last,
　　One beam by sunny beam,
You'll find yourself alone
　　And wondering . . .
　　　　　　Was it just a dream?

# THE HOBGOBBLER BOG ❧ *Dilys Evans*

The Goblin bog is full of fun—
The sun is shining high.
But don't go near when day is done
And moonlight streaks the sky.

For that's the time the Gobblers dance.
They rise up from below.
Long-legged—big-headed—eyes that never blink.
They dance and prance the whole night long,
Then right back down they sink.

Now should you hide to see them dance
And watch them hiss and boo,
'Tis certain that when night is done
You'll be a Gobbler too. . . .

# A GNOME POEM

*Susan Katz*

I wonder where a gnome might sleep.

In the glove compartment, snug and dim,
With a New Jersey map pulled up to his chin?
Might he curl up beside the computer mouse
On a mousepad mattress right here in our house?
Would he snore in a bird's nest high in a tree?
   Or could he be sharing my pillow with me,
As soon as I'm asleep?

And how would a gnome eat?

Would he use a spiderweb tablecloth? *Yes, for sure.*
Eat jellied bees' knees and wing of moth? *Hmm...probably not.*
Could he use my toothpaste cap for a cup? *nice idea.*
Would he roast an ant and gobble it up? *yuck!*
   Or, if I happen to leave the room,
Might he lick the ice cream off my spoon? *only choc*
Wouldn't that be neat? *yummy.*

And what would a gnome do?

Would he take his showers when the sprinkler's on?
Brush his teeth with a drop of dew at dawn?
For fun, might he spin in our mixing bowl?
Or hitch a ride on a passing vole?
  Or, when I'm not looking, might he watch TV
Perched on the couch right next to me?
I'd like to ask gnomes a thing or two

If only I could catch one. Wouldn't you?

# FAIRY HUNT ❧ *Ann Braybrooks*

Have you ever tried to catch a fairy?
Every summer night, I try.
But every time I think I've got one—
Oh! It's just a firefly!

21

OGRE ❧ *Rebecca Kai Dotlich*

He pounds the Earth with clubs when he is mad.
He pounds the Earth with clubs when he is sad.
Too bad. The ogre never learned to cry.
Wonder why?

23

## BACKPACK TROUBLE

*Kristine O'Connell George*

You're sitting in class when
your backpack rumbles
with odd little bulges,
and mumbly grumbles—

It's all very curious,
that's certainly true.
Just don't let him out,
whatever you do!

It's definitely a troll,
what else can I say?
Keep your backpack closed—
Beware! Stowaway!

# THE FOOTSTEP FAIRIES

*Muriel E. Windram*

The footstep fairies follow you
    Wherever you may walk,
And when you tread the grasses down,
    They push back every stalk.

They never let you see them work,
    Though you may watch for hours,
But hide themselves behind your feet,
    And in among the flowers.

Then, when you've gone along your way,
    They tug with might and main,
Till all the little blades of grass
    Are standing straight again.

# FAIRY PARACHUTE ✻ *Ann Braybrooks*

I don't always
use my wings.

Sometimes,
I crawl out
                on a branch,
twist off a leaf, hold it
    above my head,
            then

                    j
                     u
                      m
                       p

            and glide
                        and sway
                    and rock
back and forth,
            watching

                                        y
                                     l
        my friends f

while  I

        f
                o
            l
                        t
            a

                in the breeze.

# THE POINTED PEOPLE

*Rachel Field*

I don't know who they are,
But when it's shadow time
In woods where the trees crowd close,
With bristly branches crossed,
From their secret hiding places
I have seen the Pointed People
Gliding through brush and bracken.
Maybe a peakèd cap
Pricking out through the leaves,
Or a tiny pointed ear
Up-cocked, all brown and furry,
From ferns and berry brambles,
Or a pointed hoof's sharp print
Deep in the tufted moss,
And once a pointed face
That peered between the cedars,
Blinking bright eyes at me
And shaking with silent laughter.

## IMP OF EVENING ✿ *Lee Bennett Hopkins*

Imp of evening
prances
through night

chuckling
mischievously
with impish delight.

He tickles
moss ferns
until they awake,
watching their leaves
wiggle and shake.

He taunts
tired toadstools,
a sleeping fast
sprite.

Imp of evening
is *never* polite.

But when
he tires
of long puckish play

he needs
a long nap

so

*he* sleeps
the
whole
day.

# PIXIE

*Tom Robert Shields*

Teensy pixie
Teases a flea.
Tumbles a thimble of
Thistledown tea.

Frolicking pixie
Footprint free,
Ferries a prism,
Flees from a bee.

Swift, nimble pixie
Sparkles bright,
Stirs a sliver of
Sapphire night.

Sets me dreaming—
Pixie flies
Swift toward my ceiling
As sleep
        shuts
            my
                eyes.

35

## PAPA TROLL'S LULLABY

*Rebecca Kai Dotlich*

Sleep tight, dear troll,
so cute and wise;
relax your round
as gumball eyes.

Let only stars
shine on your bones,
for sun will turn
my troll to stone.

Sleep tight, dear troll,
near mountain boulder;
lay your head
on papa's shoulder.

When stars appear
it's safe to play,
but rock in papa's
arms today.

## ACKNOWLEDGMENTS ❧ *Grateful acknowledgment to the copyright holders is hereby expressed for permission to reprint the following copyrighted material. Any errors or omissions are unintended and will be corrected in future printings.*

"Fairy Hunt" and "Fairy Parachute" by Ann Braybrooks. Both copyright © 2000 by Ann Braybrooks. Used by permission of the author, who controls all rights.

"Down Below the Barlor Bridge," "Ogre," and "Papa Troll's Lullaby" by Rebecca Kai Dotlich. All copyright © 2000 by Rebecca Kai Dotlich. Printed by permission of Curtis Brown, Ltd.

"The Pointed People" by Rachel Field. Copyright © by Yale University Press, September 5, 1924; renewed © by Arthur S. Pederson, June 9, 1952, September 24, 1951. Used by permission of Radcliffe College.

"Backpack Trouble" by Kristine O'Connell George. Copyright © 2000 by Kristine O'Connell George. Used by permission of the author, who controls all rights.

"Imp of Evening" by Lee Bennett Hopkins. Copyright © 2000 by Lee Bennett Hopkins. Printed by permission of Curtis Brown, Ltd.

"Evidence" and "A Gnome Poem" by Susan Katz. Copyright © 2000 by Susan Katz. Used by permission of the author, who controls all rights.

"The Fairy Ring" by Constance Andrea Keremes. Copyright © 2000 by Constance Andrea Keremes. Used by permission of the author, who controls all rights.

"How to Tell Goblins from Elves" from *Goose Grass Rhymes* by Monica Shannon. Copyright © 1930 by Doubleday, a division of Bantam, Doubleday, Dell Publishing Group, Inc. Used by permission of Doubleday, a division of Random House, Inc.

"Pixie" by Tom Robert Shields. Copyright © 2000 by Tom Robert Shields. Used by permission of Lee Bennett Hopkins for the author, who controls all rights.

## SIMON & SCHUSTER BOOKS FOR YOUNG READERS

An imprint of Simon & Schuster Children's Publishing Division
1230 Avenue of the Americas, New York, New York 10020

Text copyright © 2000 by Dilys Evans
Illustrations copyright © 2000 by Jacqueline Rogers
All rights reserved including the right of reproduction in whole or in part in any form.
SIMON & SCHUSTER BOOKS FOR YOUNG READERS is a trademark of Simon & Schuster.
Book design by Heather Wood
The text for this book is set in Elysium Book.
Printed in Hong Kong
10 9 8 7 6 5 4 3 2 1

Library of Congress Cataloging-in-Publication Data
Fairies, trolls, & goblins galore : poems about fantastic creatures /
compiled by Dilys Evans ; illustrated by Jacqueline Rogers. —1st ed.
p. cm.
Summary : A collection of poems by a variety of authors about all types of faery folk
including trolls, gnomes, ogres, pixies, and many others.
ISBN 0-689-82352-5 (hardcover)
1. Fairy poetry, American. 2. Children's poetry, American. [1. Fairies Poetry.
2. American poetry Collections.] I. Evans. Dilys. II. Rogers, Jacqueline, ill.
PS595.F32F34 2000 811.008'0375—dc21 99-25341 CIP

**ARTIST'S NOTE** The illustrations for this book are mainly watercolor with a hint of gouache (an opaque watercolor), a touch of acrylic (for bright highlights), a fuzzing of pastel (to repair and smooth washes), and some soft color pencils (to crispen an edge or two). The watercolor is mostly applied with brushes ranging from fat to skinny, unless of course I feel the need to SPLATTER with an old toothbrush or finely spray with an airbrush.

In short, I do whatever I need to do to get the look I want, and most of the time that means crossing my fingers and asking the faery folk for help!

first edition

For Alma and Peter Barnes,
my very dearest friends.

— D.E.

For my oldest, closest pal from
first grade, Helen, and her
children, Katie and Ben, with
lots of love.

—J.R.

# THE LITTLE PEOPLE

*Dilys Evans*

Just because
You can't see me—
Doesn't mean that I'm not there!

Actually I'm right beside you.
Faery folk
Are everywhere. . . .